HERE COMES THE CAT! / СЮДА ИДЕТ КОТ!

FRANK ASCH　　　　VLADIMIR VAGIN

SCHOLASTIC INC.　NEW YORK　SCHOLASTIC HARDCOVER

Library of Congress Cataloging-in-Publication Data
Asch, Frank.
Here comes the cat!
Summary: Cat's arrival causes excitement among residents
of a mouse settlement. Text is in both English
and Russian.
[1. Friendship — Fiction. 2. Cats — Fiction.
3. Mice — Fiction. 4. Russian language materials — Bilingual]
I. Vagin, Vladimir Vasilévich, 1937–. II. Title.
PZ63.A725 1989 [E] 88-3083
ISBN 0-590-41859-9

12 11 10 9 8 7 6 5 4 3 2   9/8 0 1 2 3 4/9
Printed in the U.S.A.   36
First Scholastic printing, March 1989

In Russian,

СЮДА ИДЕТ КОТ!

means *Here Comes the Cat!*
and is pronounced
syu-DAH ee-DYOT KOT!

To my son,   To my daughter,
DEVIN   NASTIYA
—FRANK ASCH   —VLADIMIR VAGIN